MYSTIC ™

Rite of Passage

Chapter 1

1.5

2

3

4

5

6

7

CREATORS

> Giselle:
> Go easy with the metaphysical stuff. I'm still pretty new at this.

Ron Marz
Writer

Brandon Peterson
Penciler

John Dell
Inker

Andrew Crossley
Colorist

Dave Lanphear
Letterer

MYSTIC #7

Steve McNiven
Penciler

Mark Lipka
Inker

JD Smith
Colorist

CROSSGEN CHRONICLES #1

Claudio Castellini
Penciler

Caesar Rodriguez
with Andrew Crossley
CG Inkers

Michael Atiyeh
Colorist

The CrossGen Universe created by Mark Alessi & Gina M. Villa

TRADE PAPERBACK

Cover Painted by JOSEPH MICHAEL Linsner

DESIGN
Pam Davies
Dave Lanphear
Brandon Peterson
Sylvia Bretz
Troy Peteri

EDITORIAL
Tony Panaccio
Ian M. Feller
Barbara Kesel
Ron Marz
Gina M. Villa

FOREWORD

Let us watch well our beginnings,
and results will manage themselves.

Alexander Clark

It was hanging on the wall, one part inspiration and one part intimidation. It was a Joe Kubert comic book cover, art from the Silver Age. I could tell you which one, but it doesn't matter now. All that matters is that after all these years of looking at it – with its incredible composition, classic lines, and attention to detail that typified the whole damn reason I loved comics to begin with – that day it meant something more.

It was September 1999, the opening of the CrossGeneration Comics studio. The place was relatively empty. The electrical wasn't finished and you could still smell the dust from all the work the contractors were doing to get the building up to specs. We had already made our initial hires and had a plan to proceed. I had spent the better part of the last two years traveling around the country trying to make myself as smart about the comic book business as I was passionate about comic books themselves. I spoke with retailers, creators, publishers, fans, journalists – anyone whose ear I could bend. A few people took me seriously, while I'm sure others regarded me as that crazy guy from Florida who keeps buying all that comic book art. Whenever I talked to people, I'd get these incredulous looks from them, like they

thought I was unstable or in need of some medication, some therapy, or a little of both. I can't imagine what made people think that.

Oh, yeah, now I remember. I told them I wanted to start a comic book publishing company.

"In this marketplace?" was the reply more often than not. "It'll never work. Remember Valiant, Tekno, Malibu, Comico, Now, First, Eclipse, …?" The list kept growing. They were all publishers of comic books who arrived with the best of intentions, but couldn't stay in business. Now, I was adding one more publisher to the mix. Would CrossGen just wind up another footnote of a dying genre, or take its place in the lexicon of longer-term players like competitors DC, Marvel, Image, and Dark Horse? In September 1999, I knew where I wanted CrossGen's name to be placed, and ask anyone, I can be very stubborn.

So was that Kubert piece. It hung there, reminding me why I started this whole venture at the same time it was reminding me why it would be very hard for me to succeed.

Not to sound like someone's grandfather droning on about better times, but I remember comics when they meant more to people than how much they could sell them for when they got older. I remembered when comics taught us about the difference between right and wrong, about the responsibility the strong have to the weak, about what makes a hero and what makes

a villain. And as this almost subliminal education proceeded, I, and thousands like me, were entertained by our generation's *Beowulf.*

But today, a lot of those messages have been lost in a sea of graphic violence and blatant sexuality. Comics and their stories are no longer a source for inspiration and their success is largely dependent upon shock value and sensationalism. Three thousand years of heroic fantasy has taken a backseat to market fluctuations, variant covers, crossovers, and the constant killing and reviving and killing and reviving and killing and reviving of characters we used to love, but can't seem to get excited about anymore because they are being treated like disposable commodities. That old piece of art reminded me of a time when a hero didn't have to wear day-glo Spandex. A hero could have been a swashbuckling pirate, a knight astride a white mare, a sorceress from another world, an explorer, or sometimes even a benevolent prince or princess who brings peace to a war-torn land. They didn't need capes, cowls, masks, and powers. Sometimes, simply the strength of their own convictions, a little skill, and a basic weapon was all they needed.

But just as that drawing reminded me of those days, it also reminded me of how much we had to live up to. Because of all the failures that had come before us, because of all the well-intentioned neophytes who came before us, because of the slippery slope that the comic book marketplace had become, we would need to be twice as good as anything out there. We couldn't hold ourselves to a basic mission. We had to create one that was above and beyond anyone's wildest expectations, and then we had to succeed. We had to prove we could do the impossible, and do it quickly, because the comics marketplace was an impatient mistress. She wouldn't wait for us to catch up.

For that reason, our first step had to be a good one. Our beginning needed to be strong, definitive, defiant, and bold. We needed to draw our line in the sand early. We needed to think outside the box of conventional wisdom and do something so different, that at the very least, it would start people talking about us.

In a marketplace filled with brawny, muscle-bound Spandex jockeys and dark knights and mutants with powers so obscure and abstract that they'd confuse Dennis Miller, we needed a foil. We needed someone who would be reminiscent of the heroes I remembered as a kid, but fresh and lively and new for a new generation. We needed someone who would make the rest of the comics world sit up and say, "Hey, what the heck is going on over there?"

Clearly, this was a job for a woman.
Her name is Giselle.
I think you'll like her. ☻

MARK

Mark Alessi

THIS PLACE GROWS COLDER, MY FRIEND. ITS ENERGY WANES. I AM SEEKING A SOLUTION, AND EAGERLY WELCOME YOUR THOUGHTS.

IT IS NOT LIKE YOU TO BE SO TROUBLED.

SO LONG AGO, WHEN IT WAS ALL SET IN MOTION, IT WAS SO... FASCINATING IN ITS COMPLEXITY. IT SURPRISED EVEN ME. NOW THINGS ARE STATIC, WORLDS GROW COLD, AND WHAT WERE ONCE GLORIOUS FIELDS OF BATTLE LAY STILL AND BARREN.

THE PROBLEM IS NOT SIMPLY LAZY WARRIORS. THE VITAL ENERGIES ON WHICH WE ALL DEPEND ARE FADING AWAY... IT SHOULDN'T HAPPEN LIKE THIS... YET IT IS! IT IS DYING, AND THE FIRST DO NOTHING TO PREVENT IT!

BECAUSE THE FIRST DON'T UNDERSTAND. THEY HAVE NO IDEA OF THE CONNECTION BETWEEN THEIR ACTIONS AND THE WHOLE.

YES. THEY NEED...MOTIVATION. THEY MUST BE FORCED TO REIGNITE THE CYCLE...

Chapter

YET...THEY KNOW NOTHING OF MY EXISTENCE. TO DO SO WOULD *CHANGE* THEM...

WHY LOOK ONLY TO THE FIRST?

LET ME SHOW YOU A PLACE ALREADY RICH WITH MYSTERIES. GIVE THEM ANOTHER TO PONDER, AND WHAT HAS BEEN THE UNEASY RITUALISTIC ALLIANCE OF JEALOUS GUILDS SHATTERS!

THESE PEOPLE USE THE ENERGIES OF THE WHOLE TO DO MAGIC AND THEIR DAILY EXISTENCE IS POPULATED WITH MINIATURE MIRACLES. WHEN EXTRAORDINARY EVENTS ARE EVERYDAY LIFE, IT WILL TAKE A PHENOMENAL EVENT TO CAPTURE THEIR ATTENTION.

...HOW POSITIVELY *DREARY.*

Uh... ...YOUR SISTER... MY **SISTER.** MY SISTER'S PRIDED HERSELF ON BEING THE *RESPONSIBLE* ONE EVER SINCE WE WERE LITTLE GIRLS.

SHE LOCKED HERSELF AWAY AND STUDIED THE RITUALS AND SPELL CONFIGURATIONS AND WHATEVER OTHER TEDIOUS DRIVEL THEY DRILL INTO YOUR HEAD AT THE GUILD CATHEDRAL.

WHICH IS WHY SHE IS WHERE SHE IS. GENEVIEVE'S A GOOD GIRL.

BUT GOOD GIRLS STAY AT HOME WHILE THE *REST* OF US GET INVITED TO THE BEST PARTIES. LET'S FACE IT...

...THIS IS THE *LAST* PLACE YOU'D EVER FIND MY SISTER.

⇒Ahem⇐

Oh...

...LET GO!

WHAT DO YOU THINK YOU'RE *DOING?!* EMBARASSING ME IN FRONT OF MY FRIENDS *INTENTIONALLY?*

YOUR FRIENDS.

YOU CALL THAT COLLECTION OF SWELLS AND IDLERS YOUR FRIENDS...

...AND YOU FIT RIGHT IN WITH THEM.

IF YOU'RE GOING TO LIVE YOUR LIFE LIKE THAT, I CAN'T DO ANYTHING ABOUT IT. I'M DONE TAKING CARE OF YOU.

BUT DON'T RUIN THIS FOR ME, GISELLE.

I BECOME GUILD MASTER TOMORROW. THE OTHER GUILD MASTERS ARE PROBABLY IN THE CITY ALREADY.

I SHOULDN'T HAVE TO TRACK YOU DOWN TO MAKE SURE YOU'RE BEHAVING YOURSELF. I DON'T NEED SOME ELEVENTH-HOUR SCANDAL.

IN TIME NOW MEMORY, THE SEVEN CAME TOGETHER AS ONE TO DEFEND CIRESS FROM A THREAT BEYOND ALL THAT IS.

WHEN THE BEAST WAS VANQUISHED, THE SEVEN TOOK ITS ENERGY INTO THEMSELVES, AND ATTAINED SPIRITUAL LIFE EVERLASTING.

THE SPIRITS OF EACH OF THOSE MASTERS LIVE ON... PASSED DOWN THROUGH GENERATIONS OF THEIR SUCCESSORS, EACH NEW MASTER A LIVING VESSEL...

...EACH NEW MASTER THE LIVING EMBODIMENT OF THEIR GUILD'S ACCUMULATED KNOWLEDGE.

TODAY WE WITNESS THE PASSAGE. FROM WILLING DEATH COMES ETERNAL LIFE.

...THUS IT SHALL ALWAYS BE.

THUS HAS IT BEEN...

...THUS IT IS NOW...

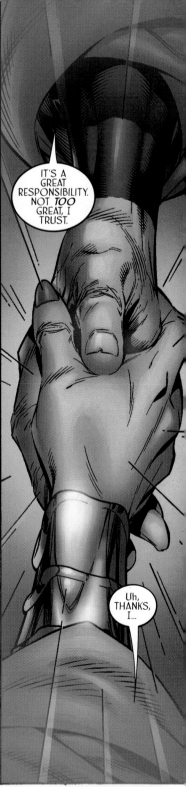

≈HHUHKK≈

THIS ISN'T *SUPPOSED* TO HAPPEN, IS IT?

SOME-THING'S WRONG.

PARDON ME, LET ME *THROUGH...*

OUT OF MY *WAY!* I HAVE TO GET...

NAROTH'S NAME, WHAT IS SHE RAVING ABOUT?

...OUTSIDE...

When CrossGen launched in May 2000, the goal was to debut with a splash. An initial release of four monthly titles seemed to be the right number, but asking fans to buy four comics to get a taste of a brand new universe of stories was asking a lot.

Hence, *CrossGen Chronicles* #1 offered an opportunity to sample the characters, worlds and stories surrounding *Mystic, Sigil, Scion* and *Meridian*. The issue featured five-page vignettes respectively showcasing each lead character and storyline. The trick was placing them all within the context of one story, so the choice was made to use the god-like beings of the CrossGen Universe, the First, as a framing device.

It also was decided that the five-page interludes would present the characters just after they'd been granted their sigils, allowing an exploration of how they reacted to those sigils. As far as the timeline was concerned, the sequences would fit betwen issues #1 and #2 of the individual series. Once the #1 issues hit the stands, perceptive readers would be able to fit together the chronology. Leaving a trail of clues for clever readers to follow would become a CrossGen hallmark.

"We used the five pages to show a bit of the fallout between Giselle and Genevieve, which is really the low point of their relationship," *Mystic* writer Ron Marz said. "The whole thing forms a really nice bridge."

Here it is, presented "in sequence" for the first time. ❧

Chapter 1.5

YOU *WHAT?*

I DON'T *KNOW* WHAT HAPPENED. THIS... *MAN* I'VE NEVER SEEN BEFORE, HE TOUCHED ME AND MY HAND FELT STRANGE, AND THEN THE SPIRITS WERE CHASING ME AND SOMEHOW...

...THEY WENT INTO ME.

YOU CAN *SEE* WHAT IT DID TO MY GUILD ROBES.

MY OWN SISTER.

...I THINK IT MIGHT HAVE SOMETHING TO DO WITH *THIS.* IT JUST... APPEARED.

I SWEAR, EVERYTHING THAT HAPPENED WAS AN ACCIDENT.

HOW *COULD* YOU, GISELLE? YOU KNOW WHAT THIS MEANS TO ME, YOU KNOW HOW LONG I'VE WANTED IT.

GENEVIEVE, *PLEASE.* I DIDN'T DO IT ON PURPOSE. I THINK...

Chapter 2

"I thought it would be much more interesting on a character level to saddle someone who didn't want all this magical power with the burden of carrying it."

— *Ron Marz*

Marz Attacks!

Chronicles contained the first display of the power Giselle inherited. The ironic thing was, it wasn't supposed to be Giselle. Originally, *Mystic* was going to star her sister Genevieve as a gifted sorceress who is granted the power of the sigil, as well as the power of all the Guild Masters, to become the heroine for the title.

But then, Marz attacked. *Mystic* scribe Ron Marz, to be exact.

"As originally envisioned in the bare-bones CrossGen 'bible' that Mark (Alessi) and Gina (Villa) had put together, Giselle was essentially Genevieve (though no one had names at that point)," explained Marz, who was one of CrossGen's first staffers. "The original vision of that book was to have someone like Genevieve as the pro-tagonist – someone magically adept and who always wanted to pursue a higher position within the world's magical hierarchy. But when we all sat down to have our brain-storming sessions for developing the CrossGen Universe in detail from Mark and Gina's guidelines, I suggested building the book around a character who was in many ways the exact opposite of what was envisioned. I thought it would be much more interesting on a character level to saddle someone who didn't want all this magical power with the burden of carrying it."

Using Giselle, a character who had absolutely no preparation for power, heroism or responsibility – let alone the desire for it – as the lead character, allowed Ron to employ a lot of themes very close to his and CrossGen founder Mark Alessi's hearts: coming of age and coming to responsibility.

"Certainly that sense of coming to responsibility was present, because we started with an inherently irrespon-sible character," Ron said. "We started with a party girl, and we're slowly building her into this sorceress supreme. It's very easy to build a character who is dutiful and proper and self-confident into a hero. You don't have as far to travel. But with Giselle, we have a great foundation for character growth against this epic backdrop."

The world Ciress, intro-duced in the previous chapter, was built to a great extent around the things *Mystic* penciler Brandon Peterson draws well, according to Ron.

"The function followed the form in this case," he added. "We built a world that took advantage of the strengths Brandon had displayed earlier in his career. The art nouveau motif is something Brandon was familiar with and excels at, so that's what we used as a base design. Then when you go to other places on the world, places where the other Guilds hold sway, we used different design sensibilities. It gives us the opportunity to play with a wide range of visuals and still create a coherent world."

The most fun for Ron in the first issue, though, was coming up with all the Guild Masters, their looks and their specialties.

"For me, the thing that made it all come together was designing the Guild Masters," he said. "That sort of tied together the whole world. Even though they were just character designs, coming up with them made the whole world seem that much more fleshed out to me. With most comics the creative team is essentially asked to conform to what already exists or to fill a

> **"It's very easy to build a character who is dutiful and proper and self-confident into a hero. You don't have as far to travel. But with Giselle, we have a great foundation for character growth against this epic backdrop."**

market niche, as opposed to being asked to create from the ground up. In this sense, *Mystic* was definitely more the exception than the rule." ↵

YEEF!

WHAT'S GOT *YOU* ALL EXCITED?

ALPHONSE!

GRROWF

NEEP!

DOWN, ALPHONSE! *BAD* GORK!

COME ON, I GOTCHA.

EVER HEAR OF A *LEASH?* THIS SQUIT HAD A BAD EXPERIENCE WITH ONE OF THOSE THINGS.

Ah, HE'S A PRETTY GOOD BOY, HE JUST GETS EXCITED.

SIT, ALPHONSE.

YOU ALMOST SEEM LIKE YOU'VE HAD A BAD EXPERIENCE, IF YOU DON'T MIND ME SAYING SO. YOU OKAY?

FINE, I JUST... I'M STILL FIGURING OUT WHAT HAPPENED TO ME, BUT IT'S NOT YOUR PROBLEM.

I NEED TO GET HOME AND LIE DOWN.

AND CHANGE MY CLOTHES.

SORRY, I HAVE TO RUN. IT WAS NICE MEETING YOU.

HANG ON...

WHAT BELONGS TO US...

...HAS BEEN STOLEN FROM US.

THIS MORNING'S RITE OF ASCENSION WAS AN AFFRONT LIKE NO OTHER IN THE HISTORY OF THE JOINED GUILDS.

...WE WHO ARE RESPONSIBLE FOR KEEPING AT BAY THAT WHICH THREATENS CIRESS, HAVE BEEN STRIPPED OF WHAT IS RIGHTFULLY OURS.

THE ETERNAL SPIRITS OF THE FOUNDERS HAVE BEEN WRENCHED FROM US.

WE GUILD MASTERS ARE LEFT WITHOUT GUIDANCE.

WHAT ARE WE GOING T DO ABOUT IT?

NO.

NO, NO, NO...

...GISELLE, *PLEASE,* DON'T EVEN ASK. YOU KNOW WHAT THE LEASE SAYS, NO NON-FAMILIAR PETS IN THE BUILDING.

AND CONSIDERING YOUR DISPOSITION ABOUT MAGIC, IT'S *OBVIOUSLY* NOT A FAMILIAR.

COME ON, CLAUDE, IT'S JUST A LITTLE SQUIT, A STRAY.

TO TELL YOU THE TRUTH, I SMUGGLED HIM IN LAST NIGHT ANYWAY.

HOW CAN YOU SAY NO TO THAT FACE?

nrf?

THAT FACE, EASY. *YOURS...*

...JUST DON'T TELL ANYONE, *OKAY?* AND IF YOU GET CAUGHT...

LEAVE YOUR NAME OUT OF IT. LIKE ALWAYS.

FOYER?

THANKS, THAT'D BE GREAT.

SO WHAT'S WITH THE...

...YOU KNOW, *THE OUTFIT?*

DON'T ASK. I JUST WANT TO GET OUT OF IT.

I GUESS, I'LL, um...

...I'LL JUST LET YOU HANDLE THAT.

I'LL BE OUTSIDE. IF YOU NEED ME.

OKAY, BYE.

I'LL BRING YOU SOME WATER.

Yeah, you do that.

IT TALKS TO ME *AND* GIVES ME ATTITUDE.

NO WONDER I'VE GOT NO USE FOR MAGIC.

LADY, LOOK, THIS IS MY JOB. DON'T MAKE IT MORE DIFFICULT, OKAY?

PERHAPS YOU'RE CONTENT TO HAVE AN UTTER NOVICE SERVE AS YOUR VESSEL.

I'M NOT.

AFF!

SO YOU EXPECT I WON'T *SHIELD* HER?

SEE WHATCHA MADE ME DO?

I'M NOT A BAD GUY...NO MORE SO THAN THE *NEXT* INFERNAL MINION... BUT I GOT A FAMILY TO FEED, SO—

NNFF

YES, AN UTTER NOVICE...

HEY!

...BUT ONE WITH A CONNECTION TO A *GREAT* SOURCE OF POWER.

Oh, THAT'S JUST GREAT. THANK YOU *VERY* MUCH.

THAT *IS* WORTHY OF MY PROTECTION.

INDEED, BUT HOW CAPABLE IS SHE?

PURSUE AN ASTRAL ATTACK!

A SPELL OF WARDING!

WHAT... WHAT ARE YOU TRYING TO TELL ME?

Chapter 3

"All the sweeping curves, the very graceful movement of the art, the fact that there are a lot of small design elements in the artwork, is all because of the art nouveau influence."

– *Brandon Peterson*

Whole Nouveau Look

Mystic penciler and CrossGen art director Brandon Peterson knew that *Mystic*, as the company's first monthly title, had to be different and daring, so he approached everything about designing the look and the characters of *Mystic* differently than he had with his other comic book work. The fact that he was even involved in some of those decisions was different in itself.

"I had a unique advantage in that I was involved in the original character creation meetings," Brandon said, sitting in a small office in CrossGen's studio. He had just finished penciling issue #11 of *Mystic*, so he had more than a year's time invested in drawing stories with Giselle and her friends (and enemies). He remembered the meetings he had with CrossGen founder Mark Alessi and *Mystic* scribe Ron Marz during which they hammered out the details of how *Mystic* would look. "Initially, one of the first visual ideas I had was an image of some magical 'other-earth' from some time in history. As we batted the ideas around, we decided we really liked the feel of 1920s Paris. When we decided that was going to be the feel of the book, the rest of the pieces fell into place pretty easily."

The easiest decision was Giselle. The team knew she had to be an attractive young female, but that didn't necessarily put her into very elite company in comics. Comic books are loaded with attractive women. Brandon knew he needed to make her different.

"We decided the lead was going to be a looker, but what kind of looker was she going to be?" Brandon remembered. "We didn't want her to look like just a swimsuit model. She needed to be pretty, yet subtly powerful – not muscular, mind you, but strong of will and intent. With that in mind, we went about designing her along those lines."

It was also decided that *Mystic* would start out partially as a story of sibling rivalry, with Giselle's sister Genevieve being a primary part of the cast. Visually, it's very difficult to portray two females in the same comic book. In many comics, most of the women look exactly the same, except for hair color and clothing. Giselle and Genevieve had to be distinct, but not too distinct since they shared the same

> ## "The look of *Mystic* is heavily based on illustration from the early part of the 20th century."

gene pool.

"We wanted to show her sister in contrast to her," Brandon said. "Genevieve needed to bear a resemblance to Giselle, but still display a definite contrast. We started with the same hair color, but distinctly different styles. Giselle was a free spirit, very daring, so her hair was long, windswept and wavy. Genevieve was the studious, responsible sister, so her hair was short and practical. It was stylish, but clearly low maintenance. Their fashion

sense was also different, as Giselle leaned toward more revealing outfits, Genevieve wore the traditional robes of her mystical Guild. Very dutiful and proper."

Designing the other characters was fun and challenging at the same time, Brandon remembered.

"For Darrow, the initial love interest, we used a classic reference, artist J.C. Leyendecker. He did a series of ads for Arrow Shirts many decades ago, and they were images of this prototypical blond-haired blue-eyed society boy," he said.

And for the general design of the book, Brandon didn't borrow much from the world of comic books at all. Instead, he borrowed from the world of classical art.

"The look of *Mystic* is heavily based on illustration from the early part of the 20th century," Brandon said. "I'm a big fan of art nouveau and the look of France, which is partially where the Nouveau Guild of magic came from. All the sweeping curves, the very graceful movement of the art, the fact that there are a lot of small design elements in the artwork, is all because of the art nouveau influence. But our biggest challenge in the book visually was to lay out the story in an interesting way through-out the seven issues where there wasn't necessarily a lot of action going on. We decided to use an illustrative, decorative style as opposed to a lot of action like *Superman*, and art nouveau helped us reflect that sensibility. With some drawing pains early on, I think we achieved what we set out to do." ↻

...THERE'S REALLY NO NEED TO BE ALARMED.

...BECAUSE WE CERTAINLY REMEMBER *YOU*, GISELLE VILLARD. WELCOME TO OUR SANCTUM.

MY FELLOW GUILD MASTERS WOULD AGREE, I'M SURE.

I ASSUME INTRODUCTIONS AREN'T NECESSARY? YOU MUST REMEMBER *US* FROM THE RITE OF ASCENSION...

YOUR SANCTUM?

BUT HOW DID YOU EVEN...?

THEY *KNOW* WHAT HAPPENED, GISELLE...

NOW THEN... ...YOU HAVE SOMETHING THAT BELONGS TO US, THOUGH I CAN'T BEGIN TO GUESS HOW YOU ACCOMPLISHED IT.

NEITHER CAN I...

...BUT I'M SURE THIS MARK IS PART OF IT.

I DON'T KNOW HOW IT GOT THERE, NOT *REALLY*, BUT I THINK IT'S WHAT DREW THE SPIRITS INTO ME.

Hmmm. I'VE NEVER SEEN ITS LIKE.

NO, NEITHER HAVE I.

THAT'S CERTAINLY NO SHAMANIC GLYPH.

IT'S NOTHING TO DO WITH ANY OF THE GUILDS, MAJOR *OR* LESSER.

I DON'T KNOW WHAT IT IS, BUT I KNOW I DON'T *WANT* IT.

I DON'T WANT THE VOICES I HEAR IN MY HEAD, I DON'T WANT ANYTHING TO DO WITH MAGIC OR THE GUILDS.

SO JUST... TAKE IT ALL BACK, OKAY?

TAKE IT BACK AND *SHE* CAN GET WHAT SHE'S ALWAYS WANTED.

THEN IT SEEMS WE *ALL* WANT THE SAME THING.

AND... YOU CAN MAKE THAT HAPPEN?

I SHOULD THINK THE COMBINED INCANTATIONS OF SEVEN...

..WELL, *SIX* GUILD MASTERS AND ONE MASTER IN WAITING...

..WILL BE MORE THAN ENOUGH TO FREE THE SPIRITS...

...*AND YOU*...

...FROM THIS SITUATION. DON'T WORRY...

...EVERYTHING WILL GO AS PLANNED.

GENEVIEVE, THE PART YOU'VE PLAYED IN THIS WON'T BE FORGOTTEN.

I THINK WE'RE READY.

...WHERE *DID YOU* COME FROM?

Big red guy with the horns brought me same time as he brought you. You don't remember?

I...

...WELL, NO.

Huh. How 'bout that.

Anyway, looks like you got, what, like six seconds before the magic brain trust comes back here and wipes you out.

So maybe you better think about putting that thing to use. Supposed to be pretty powerful, right?

Time you started being in *control* of that sigil rather than being *afraid* of it.

EVEN IF I DON'T KNOW ANYTHING ABOUT MAGIC?

YOU CAN BE THE MOST POWERFUL *MYSTIC* CIRESS HAS EVER KNOWN, GISELLE. THERE'S VAST KNOWLEDGE HERE FOR THE TAKING.

SHE HAS NO RIGHT TO IT!

AND YOU CAN DO NOTHING TO STOP HER FROM HARNESSING IT.

SINCE I'M NOT CRAZY ABOUT THE OTHER OPTION, *OKAY.*

BUT IF WE'RE GOING TO BE STUC WITH EACH OTHER...

Given life from grains of sand
A meager tool for a Master's command
When called my kind are obliged to obey
My task to dispatch a THIEF this day

UFF?!

MY DJINN!

HOW DID YOU IMAGINE YOUR CREATURE COULD RESTRAIN HER, JINAI?

EVEN IN HER IGNORANCE, SHE'S AT LEAST THEIR EQUAL.

Nice job staying in one piece this long, but I think it's time to scoot.

OHHHHHH...

Not bad as getaways go, but your landings could use a little work.

CAREFUL THERE...

Chapter 4

"The biggest attraction for me from the beginning has been that there weren't any preset parameters."

– *Andrew Crossley*

comics on the side

By issue #4, *Mystic* had turned the world on its side. Okay, actually, it only turned its own world on its side.

The start of issue #4 begins with the reader having to hold the book on its side for the first couple of pages, and then the panels actually rotate and correct their orientation by the end of page 3. Why?

It started with a phone call that *Mystic* penciler Brandon Peterson made to Ron Marz one weekend.

"He called me up at home and said, 'Hey, I have this idea I've been thinking about.' Neither one of us are big fans of the sideways spreads you sometimes see in comics. Anything that pulls you out of the comic and makes you turn the actual book is a storytelling failure. But in this case, starting the book on its side with the panels actually rotating to orient the book properly again, seemed like it fit."

The unusual layout was meant to jar the reader, since the opening sequence took place on the spirit plane, home to the eternal spirits of each Guild. It was also a chance to try something new by literally turning the world on its ear, a freedom that keeps Brandon and the art team of inker John Dell and colorist Andrew Crossley excited about *Mystic*.

> ## "Neither one of us are big fans of the sideways spreads you sometimes see in comics."

"The biggest attraction for me from the beginning has been that there weren't any preset parameters," Andrew said. "Everything was black and white when I got it – and with the help of Brandon and Mark [Alessi], I've been creating the color scheme for every new character from scratch. That's the big difference between this and the other projects I've done."

While Andrew knew early in the process how exciting working on *Mystic* would be, it took John Dell until after the first issue was printed to get the joke.

"It took me a while to find my feet, because I had never inked anyone like Brandon before," John said.

"When I got my first copy of #1, tip of the hat to production, it rocked. When I'm working on a page, I don't really *see* the work when I'm doing it. When it's printed, and I see all the pieces together, that's when it really works for me. When I get to look at it all inked and colored and printed and lettered, that's when I enjoy it the most. When I saw that first finished issue, that's when I knew it was good. That's when I knew I could send it out into the world and let other people look at it." ●

WHO...

...WHO ARE YOU?

I'M NOT GOING TO HURT YOU. I'M A FRIEND.

MY NAME IS—

FREEF!

Hn?

...AND A FACE THIS PRETTY SHOULDN'T BE STAINED WITH TEARS.

MY NAME IS *DARROW*. I'M HONORED TO MAKE YOUR ACQUAINTANCE.

I'M GISELLE. GISELLE VILLARD.

PLEASED TO MEET YOU TOO.

Um...? DARROW? IS THAT A FIRST NAME, OR A LAST NAME, OR...WHAT EXACTLY?

JUST DARROW. THAT'S ALL.

VILLARD IS A NAME I'VE HEARD BEFORE.

THE SAME VILLARD WHO WAS TO BE NOUVEAU GUILD MASTER UNTIL YESTERDAY'S RITE WAS DISRUPTED?

DOES *THAT* HAVE SOMETHING TO DO WITH HOW YOU ENDED UP HERE?

THAT'S MY SISTER, GENEVIEVE. SHE WAS *SUPPOSED* TO BE GUILD MASTER, BUT...

...oh, I'VE MADE SUCH A MESS OF THINGS.

IT CAN'T BE ALL *THAT* BAD. IF YOU TELL ME WHAT'S WRONG...

...MAYBE I CAN HELP.

THERE MUST BE QUITE A TALE TO HOW YOU CAME TO APPEAR IN AN ALLEY IN THE MIDDLE OF THE NIGHT WEARING SUCH AN...

...*INTERESTING*...

...FASHION CHOICE. YOU *CAN* TRUST ME, GISELLE.

OKAY.

OKAY, I REALLY DO NEED TO TALK TO SOME- BODY ABOUT... EVERYTHING.

BUT YOU SHOULD UNDERSTAND SOMETHING ABOUT ME FIRST.

EVEN THOUGH MY FAMILY'S ALWAYS BEEN ALLIED WITH THE NOUVEAU GUILD, I *NEVER* CARED ABOUT MAGIC.

MY SISTER'S THE ONE WHO WANTED THAT. SHE APPLIED HERSELF WHILE I DID... *OTHER* THINGS.

GEN WORKED PRETTY MUCH HER ENTIRE LIFE TO GET A CHANCE AT BECOMING GUILD MASTER. AND WHEN SHE FINALLY DID, *I* SCREWED UP HER RITE OF ASCENSION.

BECAUSE OF THIS.

95

WAKE UP, MY DEAR.

Mmmnn... WHERE'S MY...

...MY *SISTER?* WHERE'S GISELLE?

GONE, OF COURSE.

SHE ESCAPED, BECAUSE OF *YOUR* INTERVENTION.

SHE ESCAPED WITH *OUR* ETERNAL SPIRITS STILL HELD HOSTAGE WITHIN HER.

BUT WE HAVE *YOU,* GENEVIEVE, DON'T WE?

SAVE THAT TONE FOR SOMEBODY WHO'S GOING TO BE INTIMIDATED BY IT.

YOU COULD HAVE BEEN ONE OF US, YOU KNOW. YOU COULD HAVE SHARED IN THE RESPONSIBILITY OF BEING A GUILD MASTER. SHARED IN THE POWER.

BUT YOU CHOSE TO BETRAY US.

WE ATTEMPTED TO BE...

...PLEASANT...

...IN THIS MATTER.

THE POWER YOUR SISTER WIELDS IS NOT HERS.

IT WON'T BE ALLOWED TO CONTINUE.

AT ANY COST.

NO LONGER.

SKRAASH!

Oh boy! Oh boy! Oh boy!

YEAH, OKAY...

...SO THE WHOLE TALKING-TO-HERSELF THING WAS PRETTY STRANGE, AND I HAVE NO IDEA *WHAT* SHE WAS WEARING. BUT THERE *WAS* SOMETHING ABOUT HER, ALPHONSE.

ME STOPPING BY LIKE THIS, YOU THINK SHE'LL BE...

GROWF

KRUMMBLDYPUTPUTPUT

...SURPRISED?

NOW WHAT THE HELL'S *THIS* FIRST THING IN THE MORNING?

SIN5R

FRIEND OF YOURS?

NOT REALLY. I ONLY MET HIM YESTERDAY. HE'S AN ARTIST.

Ah. A BOHEMIAN.

SO YOUR DOORMAN ISN'T ON DUTY YET?

NO, CLAUDE'S NOT A FAMOUSLY EARLY RISER, ESPECIALLY WHEN HE'S HAD A DATE WITH A TALL CHARDONNAY. IT'S OKAY, I'LL JUST TAKE THE STAIRS.

NONSENSE. I'VE SEEN YOU THIS FAR, I'D BE TERRIBLY REMISS IF I DIDN'T FINISH THE JOB.

MAY I?

IT'S NOT NECESSARY, BUT IF YOU DON'T MIND...

...SURE.

HAPPY TO BE OF SERVICE.

FLOOR?

Oh, NO... *LOOK AT* THIS PLACE.

I COMPLETELY FORGOT IT WOULD BE SUCH A SHAMBLES.

THERE WAS THIS BIG RED GUY WITH HORNS AND...

...SORRY, THIS'LL JUST TAKE A MINUTE.

psst Hey, I do NOT like this guy.

SO? WHO ASKED *YOU?*

Um, WOULD YOU EXCUSE ME A MINUTE?

I'VE BEEN DYING TO GET OUT OF THIS... YOU KNOW, THIS *OUTFIT.* I'D LIKE TO GO CHANGE.

I SUSPECT YOU DON'T HAVE TO.

SORRY? I'M... NOT SURE WHAT YOU MEAN.

FROM WHAT YOU'VE SAID, I SUSPECT YOUR ATTIRE IS ACTUALLY A MAGICAL CONSTRUCT. IT CAN LIKELY BE MAGICALLY *DECONSTRUCTED*.

THIS ALMOST CERTAINLY CONNECTS YOU TO SOME SORT OF POWER SOURCE. SOMETHING *UNLIKE* THE MAGIC COMMON TO CIRESS.

I'M FAIRLY CERTAIN YOU CAN SHED YOUR CLOTHING AT WILL.

ARE *YOU* TRYING TO GET ME OUT OF MY CLOTHES?

NOTHING OF THE KIND.

I'M SAYING THIS MARK ALLOWS YOU TO CHOOSE WHATEVER RAIMENT YOU LIKE. SIMPLY PUT YOUR MIND TO IT.

YOU MEAN...

....JUST *THINK* ABOUT IT?

NO SPELL?

NO INCANTATION?

VERY NICELY DONE...

...AND A LOVELY CHOICE AS WELL.

THANK YOU. I LIKE IT TOO.

TELL ME SOMETHING. WHERE ARE YOU FROM?

NOT FROM AROUND HERE. I'M A *STRANGER*, REALLY.

Chapter 5

"I love the backgrounds, almost more than the figures. I like rendering the soft organic things — the clothing, the soft anatomy, but I'm a nut for background detail."

— John Dell

For *Mystic's* John Dell – a veteran inker whose previous assignments included a critically-acclaimed run of DC's flagship title *JLA* – *Mystic* was a homecoming. Of sorts.

"I grew up reading sci-fi and fantasy novels and comic books," Dell remembered. "But the only comic books I could find were superhero comics, so I figured those were the only kind that were made."

Once he became a professional in the industry, John found himself in the proverbial catbird seat, having been given one of the most plum assignments in comics: DC's revival of the Justice League of America, reduced to its acronym, *JLA*. This was the superhero team that housed all of DC's icons – Superman, Batman, Wonder Woman, The Flash, etc.

"*JLA* was a blast," John said. "It was every big gun DC had, and they said, 'Here's every toy we have – go play with them.' And let me tell you, that will kill an artist. They had so many things going on at once it was hard for me to even see the page sometimes."

Mystic, however, brought John back to those fantasy books he read as a youngster.

"I think if CrossGen had said straight out that they wanted me to ink a magic and mysticism title, I probably wouldn't have been into it at first," he confessed. "I was into the mainstream, but somewhere

---

"With *Mystic*, I'm able to focus on the characters, and I've gotten a lot more into the characterization than I did with *JLA*."

---

during the inking of the first issue it made me think, 'Wow, I remember this stuff. This is what I remember liking besides superhero comics.' It awakened a passion in me that I had forgotten. With *Mystic*, I'm able to focus on the characters, and I've gotten a lot more into the characterization than I did with *JLA*. I can go into Ron's office right now and scream, 'What's next? What's next?' and he'll tell me if I threaten him with tickling or blunt trauma. But I have to resist that temptation, because now I want to find out when the book is finished. It's more fun for me that way. Now, I'm enjoying the work I'm doing on *Mystic* as much if not more than the superhero stuff. I'm thinking that superheroes are what you like when you're a kid. *Mystic* is a bit more grown up."

Something else that's more grown up is the book's art nouveau influence, drawn largely from the team's enjoyment of Alphonse Mucha's work from the early 1900s.

"The Mucha element – it's fantastic – I was looking at Mucha in high school," John remembered. "I love that. The more of that the better. I love the design elements, because they add a unique flavor to the characters and their surroundings. It gives Giselle a sense of place, even though she's not quite established herself yet in her new role."

Another difference for John is the lush sense of detail in *Mystic's* backgrounds. The cityscapes, the interiors and exteriors all help Brandon and John create a world that looks more real than most comic books.

"First off, I'm anal retentive, so I'll spend nine hours doing hair, and not necessarily because I *like* to, either!" John said. "I love the backgrounds, almost more than the figures. I like rendering the soft organic things – the clothing, the soft anatomy, but I'm a nut for background detail. I like to keep the figures simple and make the environment as real as possible. I'm silly that way." ☻

GEN?

HOW DID YOU... *GET HERE?* I MEAN...

...HOW DID YOU GET AWAY?

NO THANKS TO YOU.

I HELPED YOU ESCAPE FROM THE MASTERS, BUT WHILE *I* WAS A PRISONER...

...*YOU'VE* BEEN ENTERTAINING GUESTS.

Oh. Oh, I...

...um, THIS IS DARROW.

DARROW, THIS IS MY SISTER, GENEVIEVE.

GRR

IS IT NOW?

HAVE YOU KNOWN GISELLE VERY LONG?

NO, NOT LONG AT ALL. WE ONLY MET LAST NIGHT...OR MORE TRUTHFULLY, THIS MORNING.

IT'S A PLEASURE TO MEET *YOU*.

IT SEEMS GISELLE HAD QUITE AN EXPERIENCE YESTERDAY.

YES.

YES, SHE AND I NEED TO *SPEAK* ABOUT THAT.

WELL THEN...

...I SUPPOSE I SHOULD LET YOU DO SO. I DON'T WISH TO INTRUDE.

I GUESS... THAT WOULD PROBABLY BE BEST. BUT YOU CAN COME BACK, THOUGH, RIGHT?

CERTAINLY.

VERY NICE TO HAVE MET YOU, GENEVIEVE.

Mmm.

I LOOK FORWARD TO CONTINUING WHERE WE LEFT OFF. UNTIL NEXT TIME.

NEXT TIME. DEFINITELY.

I'M SURE WE'LL BE SEEING ONE ANOTHER QUITE SOON, GISELLE.

OKAY, SORRY.

LISTEN, I KNOW I—

Oh, YOU'VE *GOT* TO BE KIDDING.

YOU'RE NOT EVEN *HOUSE-TRAINED?!*

THAT RUG WAS HAND-LOOMED IN THE DERVISH QUARTER!

BLRF

EXCUSE ME.

APPARENTLY **SOMEBODY** HAS TO GO OUTSIDE.

Shame about the rug, but what was I SUPPOSED to do? You weren't paying attention to me otherwise.

We got a problem here.

BLADDER CONTROL.

No, it's your sister. Actually, it's NOT your sister.

FIRST, YOU DIDN'T LIKE THE GUY WHO WAS KIND ENOUGH TO BRING ME HOME, *NOW* YOU DON'T LIKE MY SISTER?

SOME PET YOU ARE.

I'm telling you, there's something NOT RIGHT about her.

OOPS, WORRY ABOUT IT LATER, GISELLE.

HFF!

BLARGH!

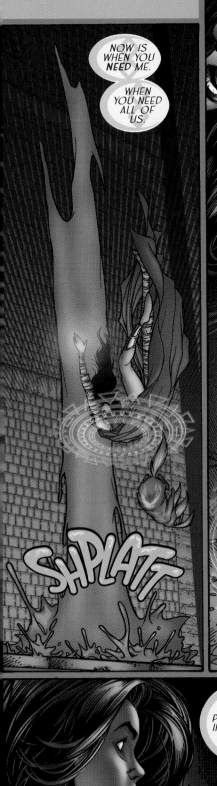

NOW IS WHEN YOU **NEED** ME.

WHEN YOU NEED ALL OF US.

SHPLATT

SO WHERE **ARE** THE REST OF YOU? WHY'S EVERYBODY ELSE SO QUIET?

OOF?

THE OTHER SIX SPIRITS? THEY REMAIN WITHIN YOU, BUT KEEP THEIR SILENCE FOR THE MOMENT.

THEY RESIST WHAT YOU REPRESENT. THEY RESENT THE CHANGE TO WHAT THEY'VE ALWAYS KNOWN.

BUT I SEE THE POSSIBILITY INHERENT IN WHAT YOU ARE.

Uh... RIGHT.

SO HAVEN'T THESE GUYS HAD ENOUGH? I MEAN, LOOK AT THEM, THEY'RE ALL JUST...

...LITTLE FELLAS.

125

1

...OFF!

YEEEEEE!

KERRASH

DAMN IT, I ACTUALLY *GO* TO THAT PLACE!

GISELLE, DON'T ALLOW YOURSELF DISTRACTIONS.

YOU HAVE A CHANCE TO BE SOMETHING... UNPRECEDENTED.

I HAVE A CHANCE TO BE *SMOTHERED!*

GROSS.

EVEN I DON'T UNDERSTAND THE FULL NATURE OF YOUR SIGIL.

BUT IT ALLOWS YOU TO CREATE A SYNTHESIS OF ALL THE MAJOR MAGICS OF CIRESS.

IF YOU'RE ABLE TO HARNESS THAT, IT COULD BE...

...SPECTACULAR.

SPLUK

SPLAP

FLUMP

Wuh-oh

AT LEAST WHEN I CONFRONT THE MASTERS I WON'T BE FALLING OUT OF MY TOP.

Well... ...we'll see.

SOMEHOW I THINK THAT'S GOING TO BE THE *LEAST* OF MY WORRIES...

Chapter 6

"When I think of magic, I see it as something that pops out from the rest of the image."

– Andrew Crossley

Colorful Characters

Ciress is a world of magic, governed by the greatest sorcerers alive. But without the efforts of Andrew Crossley, Ciress would be a pale, barren world of magician wannabes, because as colorist of *Mystic*, Andrew's the man with the magic. Instead of using line art to denote the physical manifestation of the magic spells woven on Ciress, the team decided to make use of the computer technology now available to colorists like Andrew in order to portray how magic looked on Giselle's world.

The results were, well, magical.

"When I think of magic, I see it as something that pops out from the rest of the image," Andrew explained. "If it were done with line art, it would look too much like part of the primary image. With the spells portrayed through the use of colors, it makes them look more like an other-worldly presence, like it doesn't belong there on that plane of reality."

As a result, penciler Brandon Peterson doesn't draw the spells onto the original art boards, but simply leaves space for them. Working in concert, Brandon and Andrew create and place the effects-heavy spells.

"We're not limited by a line drawing," Andrew said. "I wanted to be free to try out new things, and with the computer's capabilities, I really had a very rich palette to choose from."

As a colorist, Andrew has worked with paints and markers, but now uses the computer as his main coloring device. Contrary to popular belief, the computer actually does not do anything "automatically"

> **"I wanted to be free to try out new things, and with the computer's capabilities, I really had a very rich palette to choose from."**

to the pages. In fact, most comic book colorists who use computers work with a pen-stylus against a pressure-sensitive pad. Andrew views the computer simply as an extra tool, like a brush or a marker, with many

more capabilities to achieve a desired effect.

"I used to do some painting, some marker guides, doing the same thing I'm doing now," Andrew said. "It was a lot like coloring with watercolors, and I went right to the computer with that. I took the markers in a certain direction, but then I hit a brick wall and couldn't go any further. Now I use the computer, and it allows me to carry my inspiration a lot further than I ever could before."

Andrew says much of the work he's done on *Mystic* is influenced by fantasy novels he read when he was younger.

"I used to like the TSR books – magic and knights and sword and sorcery and dragons," he said. "I refer to a lot of the stories I read back then and the things I thought were cool. I try to think of those things when I'm doing the page, not so much to mimic what I've read, but rather to try to figure out why a particular spell is being used. What is it doing? What effect is it having?"

145

VROOOSH

...THE REST...

KRIII

DESPITE WHAT YOU BELIEVE, ALAIN, SHE'LL *NEVER* SURVIVE ALL OF THEM.

WAIT.

THEY TREAT ME LIKE A FOOL, YOU KNOW...

FHOOM

MONDRU?

...TELLING *ME* TO STAND GUARD WHILE *THEY* ACT. DIDN'T I ARM MYSELF WITH THE BOOTS OF BARTA AND GAUNTLETS OF GIMMI? THEY'VE NEVER RESPECTED—

A-*HA!*

OOP.

TRYING TO *SNEAK* UP ON ME! YOU'RE THE THIEF'S PET, *AREN'T* YOU? WHY WOULD *ANYONE* PICK SOMETHING AS MANGY AS A *SQUIT* FOR THEIR FAMILIAR?

YIIIEEE!

I HAVE *NO IDEA* WHAT THAT IS...

...BUT THE TIMING WAS RIGHT.

NG!

NOW WHERE DID THAT BURST—

...THE OTHER ONE'S FREE.

HOW COULD—

AH?!

I'LL HAVE YOUR SKULL FOR A GOBLET, YOU ACCURSED—

SHRAK

KOOM

SHE'S PRETTY RESILIENT.

RUNS IN THE FAMILY.

TELL ME, GISELLE...

153

...WHAT'S YOUR SISTER'S LIFE WORTH TO YOU?

IS IT WORTH *YOUR* LIFE?

YOURS FOR HERS, GISELLE. SURRENDER YOURSELF AND SHE LIVES. DEFY ME...

...AND I'LL *SACRIFICE* HER HERE AND NOW.

WHEN I GOT DRAGGED INTO ALL THIS I DIDN'T KNOW ANYTHING ABOUT MAGIC...

...BUT I'M *LEARNING.*

YOU DECEIVED ME...

THANKS FOR THE *LESSON!*

WHAK

YOU'RE NOT THE ONLY ONES WHO CAN MAKE DOUBLES.

HEY, SIS...

...YOU MIGHT AS WELL MAKE THEIR SANCTUM YOURS, TOO.

Chapter 7

"Just as Giselle's 'costume' consists of the ceremonial garb of her Guild, the other Guild Masters will have 'costumes' reflecting the design motif of that Guild."

*– from the notes of
Ron Marz*

Guild by Association

From the very beginning, the world of Ciress was going to be governed by magical Guilds representing a wide variety of mystical disciplines. The team assigned each Guild a symbol, a key color, and some basic characteristics. Directly from the notes of *Mystic* writer Ron Marz — written in October of 1999 — here are the original descriptions of the magic Guilds of Ciress:

Nouveau: *The Guild with which the sisters are aligned, the closest to the overall look of the world.*

Djinn: *Picture "Arabian Nights," with genies, etc. Think of the graceful curves associated with Arabian architecture and costuming.*

Dark Magi: *Black robes,* shaven pates, the kind of look we've come to associate with the darker, spookier aspects of magic. The look here should be as austere and plain as the nouveau look is beautiful. This provides the main opposition to the Nouveau Guild.

Shaman: *A more animalistic, earth-tone look. Perhaps masks are part of their regular garb, always concealing the features of the Guild members.*

Astral: *Draw inspiration from Steve Ditko's* Dr. Strange *stuff in terms of all those weird design elements. The costumes would be bizarre, the settings reminiscent of Ditko's voids, with stairs hanging in space, floating eyes, etc.*

Enchantress: *A female-only Guild, the thought here is Tibetan, because it has the* most alien, exotic quality of the various Asian motifs. But certainly elements of Chinese and Japanese design can be utilized as well.

Tantric: *A Guild with a more tantric, sexuality-based brand of magic. Their look should reflect this sexual tone, so maybe this is the venue for an aggressive display of the human body.*

Just as Giselle's "costume" consists of the ceremonial garb of her Guild, the other Guild Masters will have "costumes" reflecting the design motif of that Guild. Each Guild will also have a central cathedral as a headquarters, each a grand structure in terms of design and scope. These cathedrals will each have a design in keeping with the overall sense of the Guild as a whole. Think of these as vast, towering structures, huge edifices in which their power — both magical and political — is consolidated.

DARK MAGI   ASTRAL   DJINN   ENCHANTRESS   SHAMAN   TANTRIC   NOUVEAU

I HATE TO TELL YOU, BUT THIS AND EVERYTHING THAT GOES WITH IT ARE JUST LIKE THE ETERNAL SPIRITS. THEY'RE YOURS WHETHER YOU WANT THEM OR NOT.

BY THE WAY, LOOKS LIKE YOU'VE GOT SOME TIDYING UP TO DO.

HOUSE CLEANING BESIDES.

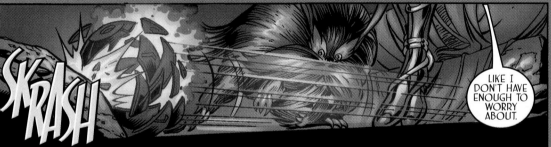

SKRASH

LIKE I DON'T HAVE ENOUGH TO WORRY ABOUT.

LOOK, GISELLE, WHAT HAPPENED *HAPPENED*. I CERTAINLY WOULDN'T HAVE CHOSEN FOR IT TO BE THIS WAY...

Yeep!

...*ESPECIALLY* MY RITE OF ASCENSION BEING RUINED AND ME NOT BECOMING GUILD MASTER.

Hmf.

AND IF THE TRUTH HAPPENS TO BE THE BIGGEST SECRET IN THE WORLD SO THE MASTERS CAN ACT LIKE NOTHING'S WRONG AND AVOID POLITICAL CHAOS...

...IT'S STILL THE *TRUTH*.

THOUGH I DON'T IMAGINE THEY'RE GOING TO JUST FORGET BEING BOOTED OUT OF THEIR CLUBHOUSE AND SENT HOME LIKE BRATTY CHILDREN.

SKRINK SKRINK

WELL.

HANDLING THIS ONE PERSONALLY RATHER THAN SENDING A LACKEY, INGRA? I'M FLATTERED.

WHAT IS IT YOU'RE CALLING YOURSELF HERE?

DARROW.

YES.

DARROW.

STILL ENGAGING IN THAT FILTHY HABIT YOU'VE PICKED UP FROM THESE PEOPLE, I SEE.

YOU KNOW I DON'T APPROVE.

I'M FINE. THANK YOU FOR ASKING.

VERY NICE TO SEE *YOU* AGAIN, TOO.

WHAT'S *THIS* SUPPOSED TO BE?

MERELY A SERVANT.

I'M... ...uh... ...MOMO.

TELL HIM TO REMOVE HIMSELF.

BOSS...?

DO AS SHE SAYS.

Oh. OKAY. THEN I'LL JUST BE, um, OUT HERE. YOU KNOW, IF YOU NEED ME.

KLIK

WHAT ABOUT HIM? DOES HE SPEAK?

ONLY WHEN I TELL HIM TO. *YOU* SHOULD REMEMBER THAT MUCH.

GISELLE?

WHAT'S GOING ON HERE?

SQUITS *DON'T* TALK.

THIS ONE *DOES,* ACTUALLY.

Is she like this all the time?

THIS IS IMPOSSIBLE.

AT FIRST I THOUGHT MAYBE HE HAD SOMETHING TO DO WITH ME GETTING AWAY FROM THE ASTRAL MASTER...

...BUT THEN I TOLD MYSELF, *"DON'T BE STUPID, HE'S A SQUIT."*

TAKE IT EASY, GEN. YOU'RE MAKING HIM NERVOUS.

I FOUND HIM...

...OR HE FOUND *ME*...

...THE NIGHT OF THAT PARTY, RIGHT BEFORE YOUR RITE. AND HE JUST STUCK AROUND.

C'MERE, SKITTER.

I still like Dirk.

HE'S ACTUALLY BEEN PRETTY HELPFUL. EXCEPT FOR CHRISTENING MY RUG.

SO HE JUST HAPPENS TO SHOW UP THE DAY BEFORE YOU GET THAT SIGIL ON YOUR PALM. AND HE *TALKS.*

YOU DON'T FIND THAT TO BE JUST A *LITTLE* BIT OF A COINCIDENCE?

Does seem kind of suspicious, doesn't it?

YOU USED TO BE ONE OF MY FAVORITES.

WHAT HAPPENED?

YOU FOUND A *NEW* FAVORITE.

YOU COULD HAVE MY FAVOR AGAIN, YOU KNOW. ONCE I WAS QUITE FOND OF YOU.

WE'D LIE TOGETHER IN MY PALACE AND LISTEN TO THE RUMBLE OF THE FALLS, LIKE DISTANT THUNDER. DO YOU REMEMBER THAT?

THINGS ARE CHANGING. OUR HOUSE HAS A CHANCE TO FINALLY ASSERT ITS DOMINANCE.

Oh, I ASSURE YOU, MY *SOLE* CONCERN IS MAKING CERTAIN YOU REMAIN FIRMLY IN POWER.

THEN WE AGREE ON *SOMETHING*.

GIVE THE PAST SOME THOUGHT. *OUR* PAST...

...*MY* PAST. PONDER THOSE WHO HAVE DISAPPOINTED ME.

OR DEFIED ME.

I'D HATE FOR YOU TO SHARE THEIR FATE.

Mm, I'M SURE YOU WOULD.

FAIR WARNING... ...I DON'T INTEND TO HAVE THIS CONVERSATION AGAIN.

YOU'RE RIGHT, WE COULD BOTH USE A BREATHER.

YOU GO TO YOUR FLAT, I'LL GO TO THE CATHEDRAL, AND I'LL COME BY YOUR PLACE AND SEE YOU TOMORROW.

DEAL.

GEN... THANKS, FOR EVERYTHING.

I SAID YOU COULD DEPEND ON ME, I MEANT IT. THAT'S WHAT SISTERS ARE FOR, RIGHT?

Carry me?

OKAY, CHUBBY...

...LET'S GO HOME.

Ooh, hey, speaking of places that need a good cleaning...

DON'T PUSH YOUR LUCK.

Hm. THAT'S NEW. I WONDER WHERE IT CAME FROM...

...AND WHO SENT IT.

Giselle

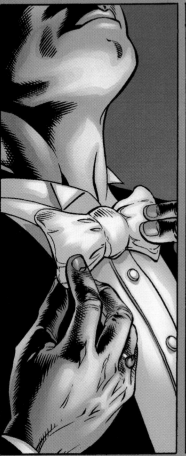

Spellbinding Covers

Making comic books is fun. Selling them is hard, which is why the cover is one of the single most important elements of the business. With a new comic book from a new company with no track record and high expectations, the cover needs to do everything but sing and dance.

Enter *Mystic* penciler Brandon Peterson.

"One of the things that I decided early on about the covers was that we were going to use a lot of art nouveau, which was popularized in the late 1800s and early 1900s by the Czech-French artist Alphonse Mucha," Brandon explained. "We named Thierry's gork Alphonse as a tribute."

One of the most recognized artists of that period, Mucha painted theater playbill posters, commercial advertisements and a variety of other posters for exhibitions, all characterized by sinuous "whiplash" lines, flowers on thin, twining stems, women with long, flowing hair, and elegantly attenuated lettering.

"His art inspired me to involve decorative borders, very controlled palettes, and a feeling of sweeping motion and beauty, as opposed to the in-your-face dynamics normally associated with comic book covers," Brandon said. "You'll see a lot of these elements in every cover, including the one Steve McNiven drew for #7. We think we've made it fit very nicely in every cover."

Brandon said his main concern with the first few covers was to establish Giselle as the lead character.

"You need to do that, especially with large ensembles, so that people can identify who the main character is at the beginning of a series," he added. "You have to give the reader an idea of what is inside the

> **"One element people don't necessarily notice from the cover is the seven ghostly skulls floating around Giselle in a circle. That is a very art nouveau element that I am very proud of."**

issue, without giving away main story points inappropriately. We sometimes don't use the cover image on the inside of the book exactly as it's portrayed, but it always gives the gist of what's inside."

On the very first cover, the main element is, of course, Giselle. She has a very naturalistic pose, showing her sigil with light streaming from it. She has a confident look on her face that is beautiful yet bold.

"We included some images surrounding her as accents," Brandon said. "For instance, her sister Genevieve, in her robes, and the Dark Magi Master as a sinister contrast to that. Even deeper in shadow, we show a mysterious figure, who looks an awful lot like Darrow. One element people don't necessarily notice from the cover is the seven ghostly skulls floating around Giselle in a circle. That is a very art nouveau element that I am very proud of. It's one of those things that may take you a couple of times looking at the cover before you catch it, but once you see it, it adds a lot to the image. The skulls symbolize the seven spirits of the legendary Guild Masters entering Giselle, which is the climax of issue #1."

The last page of the cover gallery features a bonus, a cover Brandon, John and Andrew did for the French comic fan magazine *Comic Box*. It employs many of the same elements Brandon described above. Au revoir!

BRAND
DeVries
A Crossley

BRANDO
-Jeff-06
A Crossley